For Gemk,

Whose endless supply of ideas and honest critique made this possible.

感謝 Gemk

源源不絕的靈感及誠懇的建議讓這一切成真。

The Snake's Skin

小蛇莎莉的新衣

Coleen Reddy　著

陳澤新　繪

薛慧儀　譯

三民書局

Sally the snake was lying in the sun with her brothers and sisters.
They usually liked to slither about looking for food.
Every day was always the same.
But today, something special had happened to them.

有一條蛇名叫莎莉，她正和兄弟姊妹們一起躺在地上曬太陽。
他們喜歡到處蛇行找食物，天天都一樣，沒什麼新鮮事。
但是今天呀，有一件特別的事情發生在他們身上喔！

3

Their skin had molted.

That meant their old skin had come off and their new skin was growing.

Soon they would all have beautiful new skins.

他們蛻皮了。

也就是說，他們的舊蛇皮從身上脫落，然後長出了新的蛇皮。

很快地，他們都會有漂亮的新皮了。

5

Sally's brothers and sisters had got their new skin
but Sally was still waiting for hers.
Days went by and nothing happened.
Sally was desperate for a new skin.
Her brothers and sisters started teasing her and calling her "SLOW!"

莎莉的兄弟姊妹都已經有了新蛇皮，
只有莎莉還在等她的蛇皮長出來。
日子一天天過去了，但什麼事都沒發生。
莎莉好想好想要新的蛇皮喔。
她的兄弟姊妹開始取笑她，還叫她「慢吞吞莎莉」。

Sally couldn't wait any longer.

If her new skin wouldn't grow then she would have one made.

She visited the tailor and asked him to sew a skin for her.

The tailor shook his head and said, "I don't think I can do it.

Nothing that I can sew will fit you as well as your own skin."

莎莉不想再等下去了。
如果她的新皮長不出來，那她就自己做一張好了。
於是她去找裁縫師，請他幫忙縫一張蛇皮。
裁縫師搖搖頭說：「我辦不到，我縫出來的東西，
一定不會像你自己的蛇皮那樣合身的。」

But Sally was stubborn.
She insisted that the tailor sew her a new skin.
The tailor sewed her a new skin. She tried it on.
But oh, it was too big.

但是莎莉非常堅持，
一定要裁縫師幫她縫一張新的蛇皮。
裁縫師只好縫了一張新蛇皮給她試穿看看。
但是，唉！這張蛇皮太大了。

"**Make it tighter!**" yelled stubborn Sally.
The tailor did but then it was too tight and Sally couldn't even breathe.
Sally took off the skin that the tailor had sewed and stormed out of the tailor shop.

「把它縫緊一點嘛！」莎莉倔強地喊著。
裁縫師再把蛇皮縫小一點，但是這會兒又太緊了，
莎莉穿上之後，簡直快不能呼吸了！
莎莉脫下了裁縫師縫的蛇皮，衝出裁縫店。

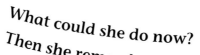

What could she do now?
Then she remembered that when people had skin problems,
they went to the beauty parlor.
Sally went to the beauty parlor and told the beautician about
her skin problem.

她現在該怎麼辦呢？

接著她想到，人類在皮膚出問題的時候，都會上美容院。

於是她便跑到美容院，告訴美容師關於她皮膚的問題。

The beautician thought for a while.

Then she said, "I recommend a sauna.

The steam will make your skin grow faster."

Sally went to the steamy sauna.

It was uncomfortable to sit in the steam

but she did it for three hours.

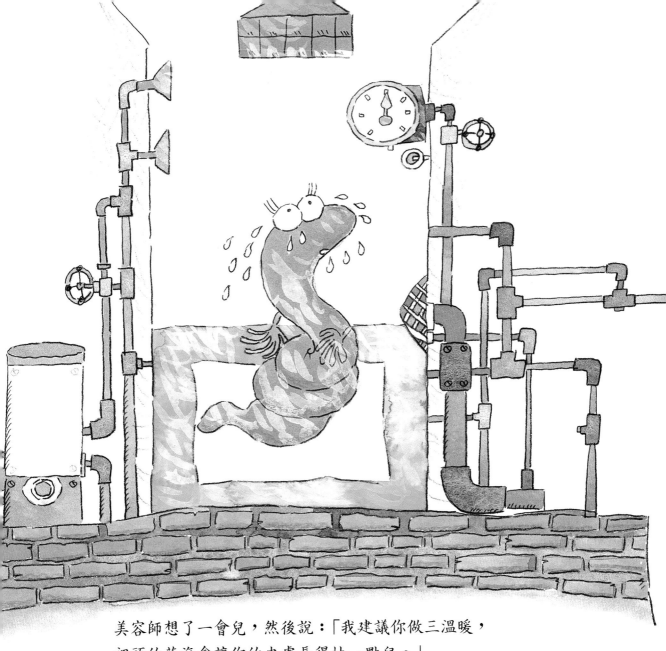

美容師想了一會兒，然後說：「我建議你做三溫暖，
裡頭的蒸汽會讓你的皮膚長得快一點兒。」
莎莉走進充滿蒸汽的三溫暖室。坐在溼熱的蒸汽裡面
真是不舒服，但她還是乖乖在裡頭坐了三個小時。

Sally came out of the sauna and still she had no new skin.
"Maybe this special soap will help. Wash yourself with this soap,"
said the beautician, beginning to worry.
Sally washed herself with the soap but still nothing happened.

莎莉從三溫暖室裡出來，仍然沒有長出新蛇皮。
「也許這種特殊的香皂會有效，用這塊香皂洗你的皮膚試試看。」
開始有些擔心的美容師說。
莎莉用這塊香皂洗自己的蛇皮，但還是什麼也沒發生！

19

"There's nothing I can do," said the beautician sadly.
"Perhaps you should go home and wait."
"**No, I won't wait forever,**" said Sally as she stormed
out of the beauty parlor.

「我沒辦法幫你了。」美容師難過地說。「也許你該回家等等看。」
「不要！我不要一直等下去嘛！」莎莉一面說，一面衝出美容院。

21

As Sally slithered home, she started crying.

What if she never got her new skin?

A butterfly heard her and asked her what was wrong.

在蛇行回家的路上，莎莉哭了起來。
要是她的新蛇皮永遠都長不出來，該怎麼辦呢？
有隻蝴蝶聽到了她的哭聲，問她怎麼了。

She told the butterfly about her skin problem.
The butterfly comforted her, "Don't cry. You shouldn't be so stubborn. You should get some sleep. I used to be an ugly caterpillar, but then I went to sleep in a cocoon and when I woke up I was a beautiful butterfly."

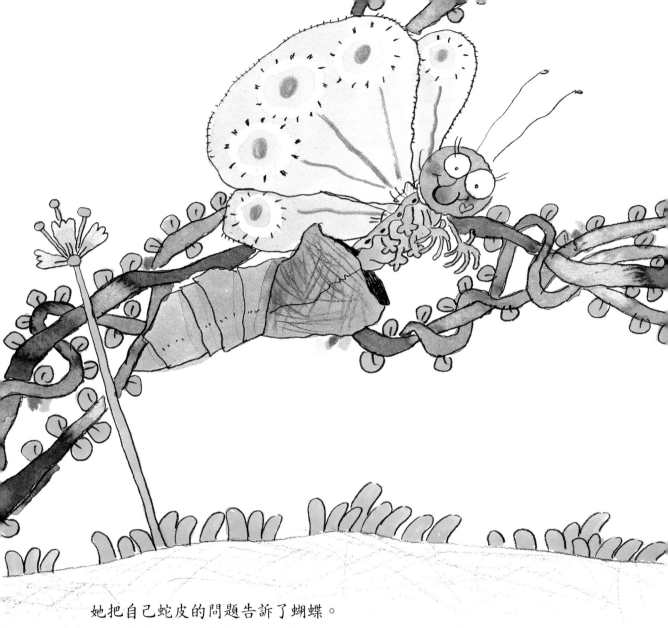

她把自己蛇皮的問題告訴了蝴蝶。
蝴蝶安慰她說：「別哭了，你也別這麼任性嘛！你應該先好好
睡一覺才對。我以前是隻醜醜的毛毛蟲，但是我在蛹裡面睡
了一大覺，醒來時就變成一隻漂亮的蝴蝶了呢！」

So Sally went home and got some sleep.
When she woke up she felt good.
But she was afraid to open her eyes.
She would be so sad if her new skin hadn't grown.

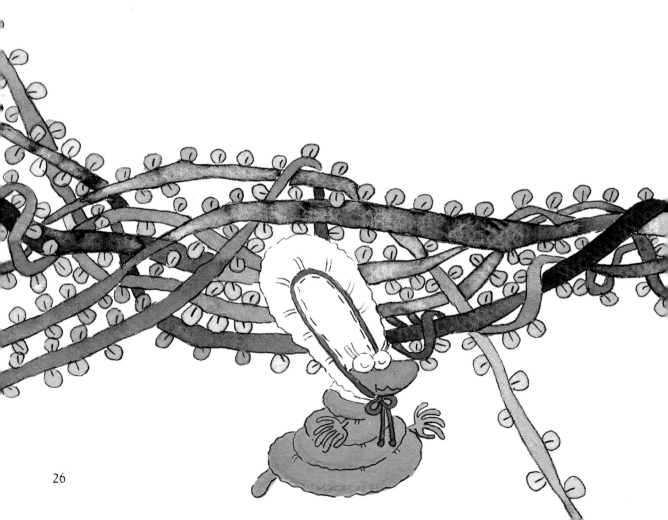

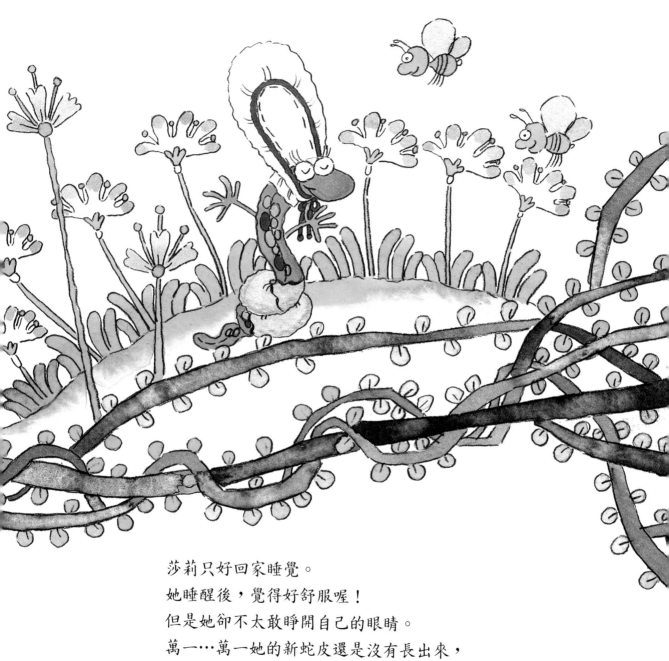

莎莉只好回家睡覺。
她睡醒後,覺得好舒服喔!
但是她卻不太敢睜開自己的眼睛。
萬一…萬一她的新蛇皮還是沒有長出來,
她一定會很難過的!

27

She opened her eyes slowly.

Sally was shocked.

She didn't know whether it was the soap or the sauna

but something strange had happened to her.

Her brothers and sisters couldn't stop looking at her.

她慢慢地睜開眼睛。

莎莉嚇了一大跳！

不知道是因為用了那塊肥皂，還是因為做了三溫暖的緣故，

有件奇怪的事情發生在她身上了！

她的兄弟姊妹也都一直盯著她看。

She got her new skin.
It was no ordinary snakeskin.
It had many beautiful colors and patterns.
Even though Sally was the last one to get her new skin,
it was the most beautiful.

Sometimes, slow is good.

她有了新的蛇皮，而且還不是普通的蛇皮喔！

上頭有許多漂亮的顏色和圖案呢！

雖然莎莉是最後一個才蛻皮的，但她的新蛇皮卻是最漂亮的。

所以說，有時候慢工才會出細活喔！

小蛇莎莉的連環新造型

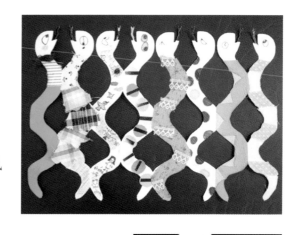

＊在做勞作之前，要記得在桌上先鋪一張紙或墊板，才不會把桌面弄得髒兮兮喔！

步驟

1. 將圖畫紙折成如左圖（寬度要相等喔）。
2. 在第一面畫上小蛇的形狀（記得圖與兩邊要有相連的地方），如左下圖。
3. 沿著畫好的形狀將整疊紙一起剪下來，如右上圖。
4. 最後，用色筆或是花紋布料裝飾小蛇，你就是小蛇莎莉專屬的小小服裝設計師囉！

生字表

 p. 2

slither [ˋslɪðə] 動 滑行

 p. 4

molt [molt] 動 蛻皮

 p. 6

desperate [ˋdɛspərɪt] 形 極渴望的
tease [tiz] 動 嘲弄，取笑

 p. 8

tailor [ˋtelə] 名 裁縫師
sew [so] 動 縫紉

 *p. 10*

stubborn [ˋstʌbən] 形 頑固的
insist [ɪnˋsɪst] 動 堅持

 *p. 12*

storm out 猛衝

 *p. 14*

beauty parlor 美容院
beautician [bjuˋtɪʃən] 名 美容師

 *p. 16*

recommend [͵rɛkəˋmɛnd] 動 推薦
sauna [ˋsɔnɑ] 名 三溫暖

 *p. 24*

comfort [ˋkʌmfət] 動 安慰
caterpillar [ˋkætə͵pɪlə] 名 毛毛蟲
cocoon [kəˋkun] 名 繭；蛹

 *p. 30*

ordinary [ˋɔrdə͵nɛrɪ] 形 普通的

33

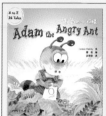

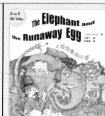

A to Z
26 Tales

二十六個妙朋友，陪你一起

愛閱雙語叢書

✿26個妙朋友系列✿

二十六個英文字母，二十六冊有趣的讀本，最適合初學英文的你！

快樂學英文！

精心錄製的雙語ＣＤ，
　　讓孩子學會正確的英文發音
用心構思的故事情節，
　　讓兒童熟悉生活中常見的單字
特別設計的親子活動，
　　讓家長和小朋友一起動動手、動動腦

波波唸翻天系列

你知道可愛的小兔子也會"碎碎唸"嗎？
波波就是這樣。
他將要告訴我們什麼有趣的故事呢？

波波的復活節／波波的西部冒險記／波波上課記／我愛你，波波
波波的下雪天／波波郊遊去／波波打球記／聖誕快樂，波波／波波的萬聖夜

共 9 本，每本均附 CD

國家圖書館出版品預行編目資料

The Snake's Skin:小蛇莎莉的新衣 / Coleen Reddy
著; 陳澤新繪; 薛慧儀譯.－－初版一刷.－－臺
北市; 三民，2003
　　面; 　公分－－(愛閱雙語叢書.二十六個妙朋
友系列) 中英對照
ISBN 957–14–3760–3　(精裝)

　1.英國語言－讀本

523.38　　　　　　　　　　　　　92008823

©　The Snake's Skin
——小蛇莎莉的新衣

著作人　Coleen Reddy
繪　圖　陳澤新
譯　者　薛慧儀
發行人　劉振強
著作財
產權人　三民書局股份有限公司
　　　　臺北市復興北路386號
發行所　三民書局股份有限公司
　　　　地址 / 臺北市復興北路386號
　　　　電話 / (02)25006600
　　　　郵撥 / 0009998–5
印刷所　三民書局股份有限公司
門市部　復北店 / 臺北市復興北路386號
　　　　重南店 / 臺北市重慶南路一段61號
初版一刷　2003年7月
　編　號　S 85652–1
　定　價　新臺幣壹佰捌拾元整
行政院新聞局登記證局版臺業字第○二○○號

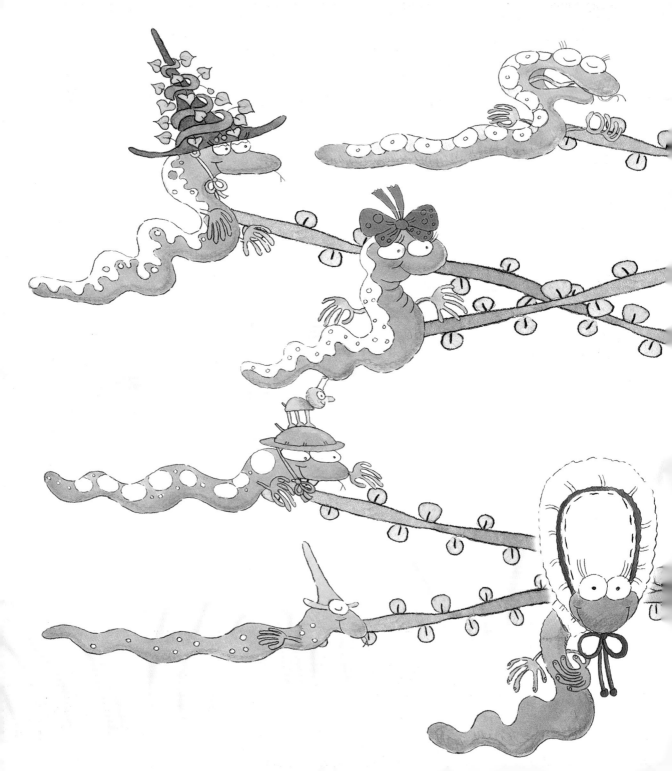